A Surrogate for the Professor: A forbidden age gap erotic romance

Willow Watkins

Published by Willow Watkins, 2024.

Table of Contents

Chapter One

"Are you sure this is a good idea?" Lexi asks from the other end of the call. "Katie, I love you, but this seems crazy."

I have to hold back a laugh, because no, I'm not sure this is a good idea. But what choice do I have? My gaze flicks to the large house that I'm currently parked in front of, and a small shiver of apprehension moves through me.

"Maybe it is crazy," I say, after taking a deep breath to steady my nerves. "But I want to do this. I could help my family out so much."

"You do realize your parents will kill you if they find out you're doing this, right?"

This time, the laugh slips out. The situation is too insane for me to be able to hold it in any longer.

"Look, I don't even know if anything will come of this, Lexi. But I do know that if I don't at least give it a try, I'll be kicking myself in the future."

Lexi sighs heavily. "Fine. But just please call me when you get out, Katie. I want to know how it went. And make sure the crazy guy you're going to see hasn't done anything to you."

I chuckle and shake my head. "I'm sure he's not crazy. But I'll call you later, okay? Love you, Lexi."

Before she can reply, I end the call. I don't want her trying to talk me out of this again. I've made up my mind, and I can be a stubborn bitch when I want to be.

With a slightly shaky hand, I reach out and open the car door, admiring his house as I get out of my car. It's one of the biggest homes in the nicest neighborhood in town. Whoever this guy is, he's obviously loaded. The house is a gorgeous, modern take on a colonial design, all white and black and huge.

"

I'm wearing a cute sundress, and I smooth down the skirt of it before taking a deep breath. *You can do this*, I tell myself, trying to calm the butterflies in my stomach.

With a final deep breath, I move to the front door. My heart is racing, and I can't stop the small voice in the back of my head screaming at me that this is a bad idea. But it's too late now. I'm already standing at his door.

I ring the bell, and it takes a moment before I hear footsteps coming closer.

When the door swings open, the man who answers it makes me suck in a breath.

"Professor Adams!" I squeak, surprise making my voice rise an octave.

Oh shit. I knew this was a bad idea.

Shawn Adams is one of the professors at my college, and he is absolutely gorgeous. Tall and well built, with tanned skin, dark hair, and deep chocolate brown eyes. He has to be at least forty-five, maybe even a little older, and I spend most of my philosophy lectures staring at him dreamily while imagining the two of us in all kinds of filthy scenarios.

This cannot be happening.

His brow furrows in confusion for a moment before his eyes widen slightly. "Katie," he says, and hearing my name in his low, smooth voice sends a shiver through me. "You're the one who emailed me."

I nod and force myself to stop staring at him.

"Yeah, I... uh..." I clear my throat and try to ignore the way his gaze makes me feel like I'm melting inside. My brain freezes, making it impossible to think of anything to say that might be helpful.

"You'd better come in," he says, letting out a sigh.

He steps back and opens the door a little wider, and I follow him into the house.

The inside is as gorgeous as the outside. High ceilings, a huge chandelier hanging in the foyer, and a staircase with an ornate wrought-iron railing. I'm surprised by how big it is. I had no idea professors earned enough to afford a place like this. Maybe I'll have to rethink my career plans for the future.

I look around, wide-eyed, and when I turn back to him, I realize he's watching me.

"I inherited this place from my parents when they passed away," he says, as if he's able to read my mind.

"Oh," I say. "I'm so sorry, Mr. Adams."

He chuckles and leads me towards the large living room area. "Given the strange circumstances we find ourselves in tonight, Katie, I think it's okay if you call me Shawn. And thank you for the condolences, but it happened fifteen years ago."

I nod and follow him into the living room, sitting down on one of the couches. The space is tastefully decorated, with a few abstract paintings hanging on the walls.

"Would you like something to drink?" he asks.

I shake my head. "No thanks. I'm fine."

He nods and sits down on the couch opposite me.

"So, Katie, obviously, there is only one way this meeting can go. I'm going to have to decline your offer of help, because there is no way in hell I can make a twenty-year-old woman put herself through what I'm asking of her. If I'm honest, I was expecting to be contacted by older women, not one of my college students. But I need to make sure that this doesn't go any further. I don't want rumors about my private life getting around campus."

I sit up straighter, my heart sinking. "What? No. Mr. Adams, I'm serious. I really want to do this. I promise I will be discreet."

I wince a little inwardly at the knowledge my best friend already knows I'm visiting some older rich guy who wants to hire a woman to be his surrogate after I found an ad online a couple of days ago. But Lexi doesn't need to know who it is. While I would hate to lie to my best friend, I also can't afford to miss out on this opportunity.

He shakes his head and leans back in his chair. "It's impossible. But I'm curious. Why would a beautiful young woman want to put herself through something like this?"

My face burns as a blush creeps up to my cheeks. He thinks I'm beautiful? The nerves in my stomach turn to a little flutter of excitement, and I swallow hard.

"Uh, well, my parents are having a bit of financial trouble at the moment, and I really want to help them out. My stepdad lost his job and can't find another one. I'm the oldest child in the family by quite a lot, and I've got four siblings who are aged between two and nine. If Dad doesn't get a job soon, we might lose the house, and I can't let that happen. This is really important to me, Mr. Ada… I mean, Shawn."

He stares at me intently, and I can see him weighing his options.

"Please," I add. "I really need this."

His gaze roams over me, and the look in his eyes sends another shiver through me. The way he's looking at me right now, like he's undressing me with his eyes, has my entire body feeling hot, and my nipples are hard beneath my dress.

Finally, he lets out a sigh and looks away. "Do you live with your family, Katie?"

I can't tell if he's considering letting me be his surrogate or if he's just making small talk, but I shake my head.

"I'm sharing a dorm room with a friend while I'm at college. My family live about two hours away. I always go and visit them when I can though. They are important to me."

"I can see that already, Katie," he says, bringing his gaze back to meet mine this time. Except the heat I saw in them earlier is gone, and he's back to being professional Mr. Adams again. "I think it's admirable that you're willing to do this for them. I really do. But it would be irresponsible for me to do this with one of my students. Ideally, I'm looking for an older woman. Perhaps one who has experienced pregnancy and childbirth before. I'm sorry, Katie."

My shoulders sag a little, and I look away, trying to hide the disappointment that washes through me. I'd really thought that maybe this could have been the answer to all my problems.

"Right, of course," I say, my voice tight with emotion. "I'm sorry for bothering you, Mr. Adams."

I get up, and he stands too.

"I really hope your stepdad finds a job soon, Katie," he says.

"Me too," I reply, forcing a smile. "Thank you for your time."

"No problem," he replies, giving me a polite smile.

He leads me out of the living room, and when we get to the front door, he holds it open. "Take care, Katie. And remember, our conversation tonight stays between us."

I walk out, and he gives me a final nod before closing the door behind me.

I let out a deep sigh and walk back towards my car. Once I'm in the driver's seat, I connect my phone to the bluetooth and dial Lexi's number before starting the engine. She answers just as I'm pulling away from Shawn's house.

"How did it go?" she asks.

"It was fine," I say, but even I can hear the defeated tone in my voice. "But it's not going to work out. The guy is looking for someone older who's already had kids."

Lexi remains quiet for a few long seconds before speaking again. "I know it's not what you want to hear, Katie, but I really do think this is for the best. Pregnancy is hard on the body, and you'd be having a complete stranger's baby. Surely that isn't what you want your first time carrying a child to be like. That's something you should experience with someone you love."

"Yeah, maybe you're right," I say.

Except he's not a complete stranger. He's the professor that I've been daydreaming about for the last two years. And the thought of carrying his baby fills me with a kind of warmth I haven't experienced before, while creating a need deep in my core that has me squirming in my seat.

I want to carry his baby more than anything, and that realization has me questioning everything I ever thought I knew about myself. Somehow, this isn't even just about the money anymore. Now I know who it is that's looking for a surrogate; it's about so much more.

"I'll be home soon, Lexi," I say, before hanging up.

I need some time alone with my thoughts on my drive home. Surely, there has to be some way I can convince Shawn to let me do this for him. I just need to come up with a plan.

Chapter Two

Shawn:

I can barely concentrate on the paper I'm grading as my thoughts drift once more back to Katie. Why did she have to be the only woman to respond to my ad so far?

The fact that she's my student complicates matters on so many levels. For a start, I don't want the news that I'm looking for a surrogate to be spread around campus. But also, she is the one and only woman who's caught my eye in a long time. I can't even begin to count the number of times I've imagined doing things to her that would get her knocked up in the good, old-fashioned kind of way.

But she's my student, and that can't happen. So I've spent the last two years trying to pretend she doesn't exist, otherwise I might be tempted to do something that could cost me my job.

And then last night, she turned up on my fucking doorstep, telling me she wants to carry my baby. It's ridiculous.

Someone should tell my dick it's a crazy idea, though. It's been painfully hard ever since Katie left my house last night.

A knock at the door to my office pulls me out of my thoughts, and before I can even call out to whoever it is, the door creaks open and Mary's face appears in the crack. I have to hold back a sigh as I force a smile on my lips and gesture for her to enter.

Mary is a fellow professor here at the college, teaching physics to the students. She must only be a couple of years younger than I am; a divorcee, if I remember correctly; and she's a pretty enough woman. Over the last couple of weeks, she's been seeking me out more and more, and if I'm not mistaken, I think she likes me as more than just a colleague.

But I'm not looking for a relationship right now. Or maybe ever. After my ex-wife just up and left me for no reason three years ago, I've had trouble trusting women. At forty-eight, I don't want all the complications that come with having a relationship. I just want a baby. That's why the idea of a surrogate seems so appealing. It's a partnership that can be managed through contracts and lawyers without messy feelings getting involved.

Or, at least, that was what I'd believed until I opened my front door last night to find Katie on my doorstep. Now I'm not so sure.

"What can I do for you, Mary?" I ask as she settles in the chair on the opposite side of my desk.

She smiles widely and tucks a lock of blonde hair behind her ear. There is a slight flush to her cheeks, and she fidgets a little in her chair as she stares at me.

"I, uh, I was just wondering if you'd like to come around to my house tonight for dinner? We've been friends for a while, and I thought it might be time for us to take the next step..."

Her voice trails off as she looks at me with a hopeful expression on her face.

I take a deep breath, gazing back at her as I try to gather my thoughts. She's nice enough, and if I wasn't so jaded about relationships, I'm sure she'd be a perfectly pleasant woman to date. I'm just not interested.

My mind flashes back to the memory of Katie practically begging me to let her have my baby last night, and my dick instantly hardens again. I clench my teeth together and force that image out of my mind. It's not like she's actually interested in me. She just needs the money to help out her family.

I turn my attention back to Mary.

"I'm sorry," I say, keeping my voice as soft as I can. "I'm just not looking to date anybody at the moment."

"Oh," she says, and her face falls. "Okay."

"It's nothing personal," I tell her, although I can't deny the twinge of guilt in my chest as her eyes water a little.

I almost sigh in relief as another knock at my door provides a welcome distraction from the awkwardness of this conversation.

"Come in," I call out.

The door opens, and my jaw drops when I see Katie standing there. After two years of avoiding her, she now seems to be making a habit of appearing at my door, whether it's at home or at work.

Her eyes flit back and forth between me and Mary, and a splash of color rises to her cheeks.

"I'm so sorry, Mr. Adams. I didn't mean to interrupt," she says.

"It's fine," Mary says as she rises from her chair. "I was just leaving, anyway."

She rushes out without another word, brushing past Katie in her eagerness to leave my office.

"Please shut the door," I tell Katie, keeping my voice professional. I've got no idea why she might be here, but seeing as she hasn't once visited my office in her two years at college, I suspect it's something to do with last night.

It's only when she does as she's told and we're alone that I notice what she's wearing. Katie is beautiful no matter what she wears, but she usually wears cute dresses that flatter her curves perfectly. But today, she's wearing denim booty shorts and a t-shirt with a neckline so low, I can almost see her belly button.

My gaze lingers on her generous cleavage a tad longer than appropriate, and I clear my throat as I pull my attention back up to her face.

"How can I help you, Katie?" I ask.

She smiles sweetly and steps further into the room, making her way to my side of the desk before perching on the edge of the wooden surface.

How have I never noticed how tanned and toned her long legs are? They would be perfect wrapped around my waist. Or my neck.

Fuck, why does my brain keep bringing every thought back to sex when it comes to Katie? I swear there is something wrong with me. I cross one leg over the other, trying to hide the obvious bulge in the front of my pants.

"I was hoping we could talk some more about last night," she says, that same sweet smile on her lips.

"I've already given you my answer, Katie," I tell her, making my voice as firm as possible. "There's nothing else to discuss."

"But, Mr. Adams, I think it would be an amazing idea. I would get the money my family needs, and you will get the baby you want. Nobody would have to know."

For a moment, a flash of guilt runs through me as I think about her family maybe losing their home. Of course I don't want that to happen. But I also can't impregnate Katie. No matter how much I might want to.

"I'm fairly certain your family and friends might notice once your pregnancy starts showing. What are you planning to tell them? That you ate one too many cakes?"

Katie laughs and shakes her head. "I was thinking I could just tell everyone it was a one-night stand, and that I decided to give the baby up for adoption. It wouldn't exactly be a lie."

I let out a long breath and pinch the bridge of my nose between my thumb and forefinger. God, she's driving me crazy. The mention of a one-night stand is just making me think again about how much I want to fuck her, and my dick is throbbing its approval at that idea.

"I have already said no, Katie. And it was wrong of you to come here today to ask again. Especially wearing an outfit like that."

Instead of getting upset at the reprimand, a bright smile spreads across her face.

"You noticed the outfit? Do you like it, Mr. Adams?"

Her hand brushes down the front of her top, drawing my attention back to her tits.

"It's hardly appropriate, Katie," I say, forcing my gaze back up to her face. I move to my feet, using the height difference to make my point, and maybe even intimidate her a little. Hopefully. "You should not have come here today, and if you don't stop asking me about the surrogacy,

I might have to bend you over this desk and give you the spanking you deserve."

Fuck. The words slipped out of my mouth before I could stop them. Having Katie so close when she's dressed so provocatively and making it clear she still wants to carry my baby is making it hard to think straight.

And while it's bad I said it, the worst thing is the moan that escapes Katie's lips at my words, and the way her eyes seem to darken a little. She gazes at me through half-closed lids, biting down on her lower lip, and her breasts rise and fall faster.

"Maybe that's what I want," she whispers, and her pupils dilate.

If I'd thought my cock had been hard before this surprising turn of events, it's nothing compared to how it is now. I'm so fucking hard that it's painful, and the fact that Katie seems to be just as aroused as I am is making it harder to remember why we shouldn't do this.

But I need to remember. She's my student. And I can't ask someone so young to put their body through the rigors of pregnancy. Katie is twenty and still has the rest of her life ahead of her.

I should just end this conversation right now. Tell her to get out and go back to her dorm room. But the words that come out of my mouth aren't any of the ones I'd just told myself I should say.

"Do you, Katie? Do you want me to bend you over and spank you?"

My voice is low and husky, and even though I'm still telling myself this is a terrible idea, I take a step closer, so our bodies are almost touching.

"Yes," she says, her voice no louder than a whisper.

My heart pounds so fast in my chest, it feels like it might explode, and all my senses seem to be on high alert. The scent of Katie's perfume is intoxicating, and when she shifts on the edge of the desk, spreading her legs a little, the unmistakable scent of her arousal hits me, and a deep groan escapes me.

"You are a naughty girl, Katie," I growl. "And do you know what happens to naughty girls?"

"They get a spanking?" she asks, and the hopeful tone in her voice is unmistakable.

My brain is so fogged with lust that I can't even find the words to respond to that question. Instead, I grab her arm and spin her around, placing a hand on her back and pushing her down over my desk. This time, when Katie moans, I'm almost certain the sound is a moan of pleasure, and the sight of her bent over, her pert little ass sticking up in the air has me clenching my hands into fists and biting down on my bottom lip.

She wriggles her ass like she's trying to tempt me further, as if she isn't enough of a temptress already.

All semblance of self-control flees me in that moment. With one hand, I grab the waist band of her shorts and tug them down, hearing the pop of the button at the front as it gets lost in my need to bare her bottom as quickly as possible. My other hand is on her back once more, holding her in place over my desk.

She's wearing a white lace thong, the material of the tiny garment barely covering anything it should. The globes of her ass cheeks are pale and round and begging to be slapped. And I don't think I've got the willpower to stop myself from leaving my handprints on her bare flesh.

I might not be able to fuck her, or fill her fertile womb with my seed. But surely it won't cause too much trouble if I just spank her. After all, I need to teach her it's not okay to come to my office to seduce me, and maybe this is how I need to make my point.

"Please, Sir," she whimpers, looking back at me over her shoulder.

I let out a low groan, then lift my hand above my head, holding it there for a second before it swooshes through the air and lands on her ass cheek with a loud cracking sound.

The noise she makes is a mixture of pleasure and pain, and I know in that split second that I'm well and truly fucked. If she doesn't have my cum dripping out of her unprotected pussy by the time she leaves my office, it will be a freaking miracle.

Chapter Three

Katie:

A delicious shiver runs through me as Shawn's hand lands on my bare skin. The sound of the slap echoes through the room, and the heat from his palm sends shock waves through me.

I never imagined he'd actually do it. But as soon as his hand is on me, spanking my bare bottom, there's no going back. The only problem is, it's not enough. The slap was just a hint of the pleasure I know his touch can bring.

"More, please, Sir," I moan, wriggling my ass, desperate for another smack.

He groans behind me and places his hand on the small of my back, holding me down. The fingers of his other hand trail across the smooth, naked skin of my butt cheeks, and his touch makes me shudder with desire.

"Is this what you wanted, Katie?" he asks, his voice husky and thick. "For me to spank your bare ass? For me to make it all red and sore, and remind you who is in charge?"

I can't believe how turned on I am by his words. This is not what I had planned when I came here today. But the minute Shawn had threatened to spank me, I knew I had to push him until he followed through. And the way my body is responding to him is better than I'd ever imagined.

I can feel the wetness soaking into the little lace thong I'm wearing, and the scent of my arousal is in the air.

"Yes," I moan.

His fingers curl around the fabric of my thong, and he pulls it upwards, the tight lace digging into my sensitive folds. I'm so turned on, and the friction of the lace rubbing against my aching flesh is driving me crazy.

"Please," I beg, not sure what it is I'm asking him for. More? Less? To fuck me, or just spank me again. I'm so overwhelmed, and the sensations he's giving me are making me dizzy.

He lets out a deep, animalistic sound that makes my knees weak, and the next thing I know, he's pulling my panties to the side and sliding his fingers through my soaking wet slit.

"Oh god," I moan, my head dropping forwards onto the desk.

Shawn's fingers rub along my slit, teasing and tormenting me. He strokes my pussy, but doesn't slip a single finger inside me. When he brushes over my clit, I cry out. I'm already so wound up that every movement of his fingers has my muscles tensing in anticipation.

When he pulls his hand away from my folds, a groan of frustration emerges from somewhere deep inside me. But the noise is soon drowned out by the cracking sound ringing through the air as he smacks my ass again. My whole body jolts at the sudden sharp sensation, and a rush of desire courses through me.

"Please," I gasp. "Please, Sir."

Shawn groans and presses himself against me, letting me feel his hardness against my thigh. His fingers brush over the heated skin of my bottom, and the gentle touch is the most exquisite form of torture.

"What is it you want, Katie?" he asks, and his voice sounds pained.

"More," I beg.

He growls and presses himself closer, grinding against me as his fingers slip between my legs, teasing and stroking. The combination of the pain from the slaps and the pleasure of his fingers has me panting and gasping, desperate for him to do something. Anything.

"Is this what you want, baby?" he asks, his voice little more than a growl. "Do you need my dick inside you?"

As he says those final words, he thrusts a finger deep into my soaked core, giving me a small taste of how good it will feel to have him filling me. In all my fantasies about Shawn in the past, I'd never once considered that he might be so dominant. So good at talking dirty to me. And it's so much better than anything I could have imagined.

Maybe that's not so surprising, though. As a virgin, I have a shocking lack of experience that could add anything special to my filthy daydreams.

"Yes," I moan, rocking back onto his finger, trying to get him to fuck me deeper. "I need your cock, Sir. I need you to fuck me raw and fill me with your cum. To put a baby inside me."

But despite my inexperience, I know exactly what I need, and I'm not afraid to beg for it.

My words obviously do something to Shawn. He begins thrusting his finger in and out at a brutal pace, making me see stars as I hurtle towards my release. I'm so wet that I can hear the digit moving in and out of my body, and the slick sound is making me hotter than I'd have ever believed possible.

"Come for me, Katie," he commands, his voice firm, and a tremor runs through me as he speaks. "Now. I want your cunt to be even wetter when I claim it with my cock and fill it with my seed."

My body obeys his command as if it was born to follow his every order, and a cry of pure ecstasy tears from my throat. Shawn's other hand closes over my mouth, muffling the sound and preventing it from carrying out into the hallways where anyone could hear.

As I clench around his fingers, I wish they were his cock. I wish I could feel the throbbing heat of his manhood buried deep inside me, and the pulsing warmth of his cum as it coats my unprotected womb.

I know it's wrong, and I shouldn't want it. But the thought of him putting a baby in me is making the orgasm feel that much more intense, and as the pleasure fades, I can only hope that he will take what he wants. That he'll fuck me without a condom.

I don't give a damn about the money anymore. I just need him to claim my innocence and knock me up. I need him to own my body and fill it with his seed.

Shawn groans, the sound rumbling deep in his chest, and his hard cock presses into my thigh. I can feel him throbbing through the rough material of his pants, and it makes my heart skip a beat.

"Fuck," he growls, and his fingers pull free from my pussy, dragging over my sensitive flesh.

My body is trembling, and I'm panting as the aftershocks of my orgasm make me dizzy and weak.

"Please," I whimper, not wanting him to stop. I'm still horny, still desperate for more, and I'm hoping he can sense it.

"Turn over and lay on your back on my desk. And spread your legs for me like a good girl."

The words are rough, and the order is given with such authority that I can't help but do as he tells me. My body responds automatically, and I turn around, perching on the edge of the desk and lowering myself back as my thighs part.

His gaze roams over my body, and he licks his lips, staring hungrily at the place between my legs. At the same time, his hands are on his belt, working the buckle open with frenzied movements. Now the bulge in his pants seems huge, and I hold my breath as I wait for him to free his cock.

My heartbeat seems to echo through the room, and I'm certain he can hear it. But I'm not nervous. The excitement I'm feeling is so strong, it's almost overwhelming.

"Do you have any idea how gorgeous you are, Katie?" he murmurs, pushing his pants down, revealing his boxers and the hardness beneath. "Your body is a thing of beauty. You have no idea how much I want to claim you. I've been wanting this for so fucking long."

My eyes widen, and my breathing becomes erratic. I want to say something, but the words won't come. I hadn't realized Shawn had been fighting this attraction, too. I'd thought I was the only one feeling infatuated.

It's such a relief to know he's just as desperate as I am.

I can't keep my eyes off him as he pulls his boxers down, finally freeing his impressive length. I've never seen a naked man in real life before, and Shawn's cock is far bigger than I could have expected. My breath hitches in my throat, and I swallow hard.

I'm not sure what's going to happen now.

"Fuck, baby," he groans, staring at me like he's trying to memorize every inch of my body. "I'm going to make you mine. I'm going to take that tight little cunt and fuck it hard."

I nod, and my thighs open wider in response to his words, inviting him closer.

"Tell me you want that, Katie. Tell me you want my big, thick cock inside you. I'm not going to fuck you until I'm certain you want it."

His hands curl around his length, and he pumps up and down, making me watch him. The sight is so arousing, it makes me whimper.

"I want it," I say, my voice breathy and needy. "I want you inside me, Sir."

He moves closer, his gaze locked on my pussy.

"I'm going to put a baby inside you, Katie," he growls, leaning over and gripping my hips, tugging me down the desk so the wet heat of my pussy is pressed against the throbbing hardness of his cock. "I'm going to make that little womb swell with my seed and fill you with my child."

The promise in his words has me whimpering, and a tremor runs through me at the idea of carrying his baby.

"Please," I moan, wrapping my legs around his waist and tilting my hips up, so his length is nestled against my wet heat.

He groans and slides his cock up and down, rubbing the underside along my sensitive clit. I cry out at the intense sensation, and he clamps his hand over my mouth again.

"Be quiet, Katie," he growls, continuing to tease me with the head of his manhood.

His movements are torturously slow, and I'm not sure how much more I can take. It's like he's making me suffer for not following his rules earlier. Like he's punishing me by making me so fucking desperate to feel his huge cock inside me. I want to beg him, but his hand over my mouth would only muffle my words, and I can't deny the arousal it brings.

After a few more moments, his other hand closes around the base of his cock, and he positions the tip at my entrance. My whole body is trembling with need, and a low moan emerges from the back of my throat.

I need him to do it.

To take my innocence and fuck me. To make me his and fill me with his seed.

With his eyes locked on mine, Shawn begins to push forwards.

I expect him to be gentle.

I'm very, very wrong.

In one sharp, hard thrust, he impales me with his cock, and the pain is enough to make me cry out, the sound muffled by his palm.

But the pain fades quickly, leaving only a dull ache and a sense of fullness. I've never felt anything like this. I never could have imagined how good it would feel to have him inside me, stretching me, and filling me.

He growls, the sound deep and animalistic, and his hips snap forwards again, making me whimper and clench around him.

"You're so fucking tight, baby," he groans, his eyes closed, his expression blissful.

The look of pleasure on his face only heightens the sensations coursing through me.

Shawn is enjoying this, and I love knowing that I'm the one making him feel so good.

He brings his hand away from my mouth, and his grip on my hip tightens while he holds me in place and thrusts in and out, pounding my pussy with his thick, hard cock. The pleasure is more intense than I could ever have dreamed. I can feel him everywhere, his thick flesh reaching so deep inside me that it's hard to catch my breath.

And it feels incredible.

"Oh, god," I moan, my nails digging into the edge of the desk as Shawn's thrusts become more frantic. "Don't stop."

He growls, his cock slamming into me at a furious pace. He's taking what he wants, using my body, and it's the most exhilarating thing I've ever experienced.

I can feel the familiar pressure building inside me again, and the pleasure is making me light-headed.

"You feel so fucking good," he groans, his hips jerking erratically as he loses himself in the pleasure.

The sound of his voice sends shivers down my spine, and my core clenches around him.

"So do you," I moan, clinging to the desk for dear life.

I can barely form a coherent thought as he continues to fuck me hard, his length stretching me and filling me in a way that makes me feel complete.

"I'm going to come, Katie," he says, his voice strained.

"Please," I gasp, feeling a rush of excitement at the thought of him spilling his seed inside me.

"Fuck, yes," he growls, his hips jerking wildly as he empties himself deep inside my body.

The feel of his cock throbbing as he comes is enough to send me over the edge, and my pussy clenches around him as a wave of pleasure crashes over me. I'm moaning and gasping, my nails digging into the wood of his desk.

As I start to come down from the high, Shawn is still inside me. I can feel his cock twitching as the last drops of his cum spill out into my unprotected pussy. The sensation is indescribable, and I can't believe how amazing it is to be joined so deeply with him.

Shawn leans down, kissing me deeply and passionately. It's a hungry kiss, full of need and desire. And I can't get enough of it.

When he finally breaks the kiss, he rests his forehead against mine, both of us breathing heavily.

"I've wanted to do that for so long," he murmurs. "But it was still wrong of me to give in to temptation like that. Shit."

He slowly pulls out of me and moves away, his body language suddenly tense. He turns and begins pulling up his pants, and the movement jolts me back into reality.

He's regretting it.

Fuck.

Chapter Four

Shawn:

"I don't regret it," Katie says, standing up from my desk with no clothes on her lower half. She folds her arms across her chest and juts out her chin in a defiant way that is such a contrast to the submissiveness she showed when I was spanking and fucking her.

Just thinking about it again sends a whirlwind of emotions through me. Guilt and shame are there, telling me what I piece of shit I am for fucking a student on the desk in my office. But there is an overwhelming amount of arousal, too. God, the arousal is like a fire that burns through me, making it impossible to think straight.

I want to do it all over again.

But I can't.

No matter how much my cock aches and throbs to take her again, I have to keep control of myself.

"It's not that I regret it, Katie," I say, trying to be diplomatic. "It was an amazing experience. But it's one that shouldn't have happened. One that can't happen again. Even if we both really want it."

Katie steps closer, reaching up to stroke my cheek with the gentlest of touches. "Do you want it, Sir?" she asks in a small voice.

I grit my teeth together, and even though she must be able to feel the way my jaw tenses, she doesn't stop touching me.

"More than anything," I confess, even though that's something that should not be said aloud. "But I'm your professor. Your teacher. There are so many reasons why we shouldn't do this. You're so much younger than me, and you could get kicked out of college. I could lose my job."

But even as I say the words, I know I'm fighting a losing battle. I know how badly I want her.

How badly I want to claim her.

To mark her as mine.

"I won't tell anyone," she promises, and the softness of her voice makes me believe her. "Besides, what if I'm already pregnant?"

I swallow hard, the thought making my heart race and my cock throb. Unable to resist, I reach out and slide a hand between her thighs, feeling the way my sticky load leaks from her opening. The touch is intimate, and I should pull away, but the temptation is too great.

"What would you do about college if you were pregnant?" I ask. A wide smile spreads across her face and I shake my head. "Not that I'm saying we are definitely going to do this, Katie. I just want to discuss options."

I idly tease her pussy with my fingers as we talk, watching the way a blush decorates her cheeks while her breathing grows ragged once more.

"I finish in the fall," she says, her voice a little shaky. "So I'll be done with it before the baby comes. It's perfect timing. I can just take a few months off before I start looking for a job. We'll only have to sneak around for a couple of months, and then we'll be safe to do whatever we want together."

It really is perfect timing, and I'm not sure whether to be happy about that or not. I was hoping for something concrete to stop us from doing this. Something that's a lot stronger than my own self-control.

But my feelings for her would only complicate matters if she were my surrogate, anyway. She's the first woman I've felt anything for since my ex-wife left, and it will be hard to let her walk away once the baby is born.

This whole thing is a fucking mess, and part of me wishes that she'd never turned up on my doorstep last night. Now it feels like we're in too deep. Like it's just inevitable that she'll be my surrogate at this point.

Katie begins squirming, and it's only then I realize I'm still teasing the sensitive flesh between her thighs while I'm lost in my thoughts.

"If we do this, I would want to set up a contract with my lawyer to make sure we're both protected. And I would want you to go to the doctor to get tested for any diseases, as well as getting a pregnancy test done as soon as possible to make sure you're not already pregnant."

The look of hope that had been on her face quickly disappears to be replaced by a hurt expression.

"I'm sorry," I continue. "I don't mean to be an asshole. But if I'm going to be paying you that much money to be a surrogate, then I would want to make sure the baby is definitely mine."

"I'm not pregnant already," she says in a small voice, her eyes on mine. "And I don't have any sexually transmitted diseases, either. I can promise you that."

"How can you be sure, though?" I ask. "What if someone you had sex with had an illness and didn't tell you about it? What if you used contraception, and it didn't work? These are things we need to consider, baby, and it's best to get you checked out at the doctor's to make sure."

Katie's face is bright red now, and that defiant tilt of her head is back.

"I will happily go to the doctor and take whatever tests you require, Shawn. And you can come with me to make sure that everything is legitimate. I understand you deserve that when you'll be paying me so much money to do this for you. But the reason I'm so sure that I'm clean and not already pregnant is because this is my first time. Before today, I never went any further than making out with someone."

Her words stun me, and I blink rapidly as I try to process what she just told me. She was a virgin? And I just roughly took her innocence in my office?

"Fuck," I mutter, pulling my hand away from her pussy and scooping her up in my arms. I sit in my chair and lower her down into my lap. "I'm so sorry. If I'd known, I would have been more gentle with you. It just honestly never occurred to me that you would have waited so long."

Her blush deepens and she shrugs. "Once I got to college, I only ever had eyes for one man. Nobody else ever compared to you, Sir."

She lunges forward, her lips connecting with mine in a hungry kiss. The moment our lips touch, the same spark of electricity that I've always felt with her is back. I can't resist her. My hands wrap around her waist and hold her tightly, pulling her against me.

I need her.

I need her more than I've ever needed anything.

The taste of her, the scent of her, the feel of her skin under my fingertips... it's intoxicating.

When she finally pulls away, her chest heaving and her cheeks flushed, her lips are swollen and her eyes are filled with desire.

"So you'll do it?" she asks, a hopeful note in her voice. "You'll use me as a surrogate?"

I let out a heavy sigh. "I will," I concede, my mind racing as I try to figure out what the hell we're going to do. "I'm still going to get you tested, but as far as I'm concerned, it's a done deal. All the tests and paperwork are just to make sure you are protected through all of this. Okay?"

A look of pure joy passes over her face and she throws her arms around my neck, hugging me tightly.

"Thank you," she whispers, her breath hot against my ear. "I promise I won't let you down. I'll take good care of your baby, Sir. You can count on me."

"I know you will," I reply, stroking her hair as she nuzzles against my chest.

This is a terrible idea. I know that. But it's an idea I can't bring myself to fight. Not with the way she's making me feel right now.

I'm putting myself and Katie at risk by doing this, but the reward will be worth it.

Having a baby is all I've ever wanted. And I have to admit, the idea of being able to breed the young woman I've been crazy about for the last two years seems a hell of a lot more appealing than going through IVF with a complete stranger.

Maybe it's selfish, but I'm just not strong enough to let this chance slip away.

Katie's body is pressed against mine, and it's impossible to ignore the growing heat between her legs.

I gently push her thighs apart and slide my fingertips up the inside of her leg. She shivers in my lap, and a small whimper escapes her lips.

"Are you sore, baby?" I ask. "You must be. I wasn't exactly gentle with you."

She wriggles, her plump ass cheeks grinding against my cock, which is already stirring back to life. But I ignore it for now. Katie needs a more gentle and loving touch.

"I'm a little sore," she admits, while eagerly spreading her thighs wider for me. "But it feels kind of nice. Like I just had the best sex of my life."

The corners of her lips quirk upwards into a playful grin, and I laugh. "I feel like the bar is pretty low, though, seeing as it was also the only time you've had sex. But I promise you, next time I'll go slow and show you how amazing it can really feel, baby."

"Mmm, yes please," she purrs, her eyes locked on mine, a heated expression on her face.

My fingers trail higher up her leg, and I brush them over her slit, feeling her wetness coat the digits. She gasps, her eyelids fluttering closed.

"Does it turn you on to think about me fucking you again, baby?" I ask, teasing her opening and circling her clit. "To think about me filling you with another load of cum?"

She bites her lip and nods, her hips rocking gently against my hand. With each movement, her ass rubs against my dick and I have to hold back a groan. If she keeps doing that, she's going to make me shoot my load inside my pants.

I continue circling her clit with the pad of my finger, and she gasps. Her eyes are half-lidded, her lips parted, and her chest is heaving.

"Are you thinking about it?" I ask, leaning in to whisper in her ear. "About how it felt when I thrust inside you, stretching your tight little pussy and filling you up with my thick cock?"

"Oh, god, yes," she moans, her hips bucking. "It felt so good, Sir."

"Are you thinking about how good it felt when I came inside you?" I press.

"Yes," she whimpers, her eyes squeezing shut.

I can tell she's getting close, so I slip two fingers inside her, keeping my movements steady and my pace even as I thrust the digits in and out of her. She's grinding herself against my fingers, her breath coming in short gasps, and her thighs trembling.

"Come for me, baby," I urge. "Show me how much you like the thought of me breeding you."

That's all it takes to send her over the edge, and she lets out a cry as her body tenses, her pussy clenching around my fingers. Her hips rock erratically, and she shudders in my lap, her body convulsing with pleasure.

It's the hottest thing I've ever seen, and my dick is so hard it hurts.

As Katie starts to come down from her orgasm, her body relaxing and her breathing slowing, I slowly pull my fingers from her. She makes a disappointed sound at the loss of contact, but her eyelids flutter open and she smiles up at me.

"Thank you," she murmurs, her cheeks flushed and her lips swollen from our kisses. "That was incredible."

"It's a pleasure," I say, giving her a gentle kiss.

And I mean it.

I could happily do this for her every day.

It might be a dangerous game that we're playing, but right now, I can't bring myself to care.

Not with her soft, supple body pressed against mine.

Not when I know how good she feels.

Not when she's offering me everything I've ever wanted.

This is wrong. So wrong.

But it's too late to turn back now. And deep down, I'm not sure I want to.

Chapter Five

Katie:

It's been a week since the day Shawn took my virginity in his office, and while I wish we'd been intimate again during that time, it hasn't happened yet. He's been insisting that we have to wait until after all the contracts are signed and I've visited the doctor.

At least I haven't got much longer to wait. We went to visit his lawyer during lunch yesterday and dealt with all the paperwork, and my doctor's appointment is after my final lecture today. So we should be free to continue with our plans to get me knocked up as quickly as possible by the end of today, all going well.

Just thinking about it sends a ripple of warmth through my body. I can't wait for Shawn to fill me up again, to claim me and make me his. To breed me and make a baby.

The thought has dominated all of my fantasies over the last week.

"Are you even going to eat any of that?" Lexi asks, giving me a gentle nudge with her elbow. "What's got into you lately? It seems like you're always in your own little world these days."

My face grows hot and I look down at my plate, wrinkling my nose at the unappetizing slice of pizza and side salad. A wave of nausea washes over me for a moment, but quickly disappears. They really need to improve the food they offer on campus. This salad looks like it's been hanging around in the kitchen for a few days and the edges of the lettuce leaves are turning brown.

I push the tray away and focus on my best friend instead.

Guilt stabs at my heart as I realize I've been neglecting my friendship with Lexi. Even during the evenings, when we're in the dorm room we share, I'm more interested in my phone and my text conversations with Shawn.

Every time my phone beeps with a notification, it makes my heart flutter excitedly, and I eagerly snatch it up to read his message. He's been keeping in contact with me constantly over the last week, and I feel like we've really connected. I'm so damn excited about being able to spend proper time with him after I've been to the doctor later. But then I know I'll probably just be neglecting my best friend even more then, because I won't even be at the dorm with her.

"I'm sorry," I say with a sigh. "I guess I have been a little bit distant lately."

She nods and flashes me a grin. "I think I know why, though. With the way you've been grinning like a fool whenever you're looking at your phone these days, I'm starting to think you've got a crush on someone."

Lexi gives me another playful nudge, and I laugh and roll my eyes. "It's just my mom that's messaging me. She keeps sending me cat videos she finds online. Who wouldn't be smiling when looking at things like that?"

She stares at me with a disbelieving expression on her face, but I don't look away. It's kind of the truth, at least. My mom has only just somehow stumbled onto the world of cute cat videos on the internet, and she does send me a few each day.

"You know I'm not going to believe that, right?" Lexi says.

I shrug, and she shakes her head and goes back to eating her lunch. I know she doesn't believe me, but she isn't going to press the issue. It's a relief. I hate having to lie to her.

I go back to looking down at my tray of food, thinking I really should eat something. After all, I've got to keep my strength up if I'm going to be getting pregnant soon. But I'm hit with another wave of nausea, and this one is much more intense than the last.

"I don't feel so good," I say, as I quickly stand.

Lexi looks up at me with concern. "Are you okay?"

"I think I just need some fresh air," I reply. "I'll see you in class."

I quickly leave the table and rush outside. The cool breeze helps to soothe my heated skin, but my stomach is churning, and I think I'm going to throw up.

I walk around to the back of the building and find an empty bench. It's secluded here, and it's the perfect spot to have a few minutes alone and calm my stomach. So I sit down and take a few deep breaths, trying to focus on the view in front of me. The trees are in full bloom, the lush green leaves swaying gently in the breeze. Birds are singing in the distance, and there's the faint hum of chatter from students passing by. It's all so beautiful, and it's calming.

I close my eyes and take a deep breath, letting the fresh air fill my lungs.

I'm going to be fine. I'm not going to throw up.

What the hell is wrong with me today?

My eyes snap open as a thought pops into my head. Surely I can't be pregnant already. And even if I was, would I even be showing symptoms yet? I can't remember. My only experience with morning sickness was watching my mom go through it while she was carrying my younger brothers and sisters, and as far as I can remember, she never suffered from it until later in the pregnancy.

It can't be that. But that doesn't stop the excited flutter in my stomach, which then only seems to make me feel nauseous again.

Maybe I should go and see Shawn and tell him what's going on. If there is a chance I might be pregnant, he'd want to know about it straight away.

My hands are shaking as I grab my bag and make my way to his office. It's in a different building on the other side of the campus, but I'm so distracted that it feels like only seconds have passed before I'm standing outside his door. Daydreams about being pregnant with his child are filling my mind, along with plenty of images of me, him and the baby together.

I shake my head, trying to rid those thoughts. As much as I might want it, I won't be around to take care of the baby. I'm just a surrogate, and my end of the deal will be over once the baby is born. Blinking back the tears that suddenly sting my eyes, I push the sudden feeling of sadness down, and focus on the fact that at least I'll be giving Shawn something incredibly special.

I knock on his office door, and I can't help but smile as he tells me to enter. I step inside, and when his gaze locks with mine, a wave of heat rushes through my body.

"Katie," he says, standing from his desk. "Is everything okay? What are you doing here?"

"I... uh..." I clear my throat and try again. "I don't know. I don't feel well."

He frowns. "Have you seen the doctor yet?"

"No. My appointment isn't until later today. But I felt sick, and... well, I thought maybe..." I trail off.

He steps around the desk and walks over to me, putting his arm around my waist. His touch is comforting and I lean into him, inhaling the familiar scent of his aftershave.

"Maybe you are pregnant?" he finishes for me, and I nod. "There's a chance, I suppose. I think it might be too early to tell for sure, but we can mention it to the doctor later. He might be able to figure out what's going on."

He guides me over to the couch and sits down before tugging me into his lap. I let him maneuver me so that my head is resting on his chest and his arms are wrapped tightly around me. He presses a kiss to the top of my head, and a feeling of contentment washes over me.

This is where I belong. Here, in his arms. It just feels so right. And knowing that his baby might already be growing inside me is just making this feel even more perfect.

"How are you feeling now, baby?" he asks. "Still feeling sick?"

I shake my head and turn to nuzzle against his neck. "No. I'm fine now."

"Good."

I can feel his body reacting to my closeness, his cock growing hard beneath me. The knowledge that he wants me as badly as I want him sends a rush of arousal through my body.

I can't help but squirm in his lap, wiggling my ass against his cock, and he lets out a low groan.

"Baby, you've got to stop doing that," he says, his voice strained.

"Why?" I ask, giving him a coy smile.

"Because you're going to make me come in my pants. And I haven't done that since I was a teenager and unable to control myself."

The words are like a challenge, and I reach a hand between us, rubbing the growing bulge in his pants. He lets out a deep groan, and I feel his cock twitch.

"Fuck, Katie," he groans, his hips rocking against my hand. "You're killing me here."

"Do you want me to stop?" I ask, biting my lip.

"No, baby. Don't stop. Maybe if you make me come, I'll finally get some relief from this never-ending need I've been feeling ever since I felt your hot little pussy milking my dick."

With his encouragement, I unbutton his pants and slip my hand inside, wrapping my fingers around his shaft. He's so hard and thick, but his skin is soft and silky smooth.

I can't wait to feel him inside me again.

"That's it, baby," he groans, his hips rocking upwards. "Jerk my cock."

My eyes lock with his, and I watch his face as I continue stroking him. He's panting, his lips parted, and his eyes filled with desire. I love the effect I have on him. I love that I'm the one who's making him feel this way.

"That's it," he groans. "Just like that."

His hips are rocking in time with my strokes, and I can tell he's getting close. I pick up the pace, tightening my grip slightly, and his cock throbs in my hand.

"Oh fuck, Katie," he gasps. "I'm gonna come."

He pulls his shirt up just in time before his cock explodes, ropes of cum shooting out and coating his stomach and chest.

It's the hottest thing I've ever seen.

After he finishes, I let go of his softening cock and stare down at the mess I've made. I can't resist running my finger through a pool of his cum on his abs, and then bring my finger to my mouth, licking it clean.

His eyes widen, and he looks at me with awe. "You're something else, you know that?"

I give him a shy smile. "In a good way?"

"The best way." He kisses me, his lips lingering on mine for a moment.

When he pulls back, my attention drifts down to his torso once more, and the mess that coats it. I slip down from Shawn's lap and settle on my knees in front of him before leaning closer and lapping up a drop of the sticky liquid with my tongue.

Shawn groans as he watches me, bringing his hand up to run his fingers through my hair.

I glance up at him from my position on my knees, a playful grin forming on my lips. "I didn't get to eat lunch because I wasn't feeling good, Sir. But I'm much better now and suddenly feeling ever so hungry. Do you mind if I finish cleaning you up?"

"Be my guest, baby," he says, his voice husky.

So I do just that, slowly licking and sucking his skin clean, savoring his masculine flavor. He tastes better than any meal I've ever had.

After I've lapped up the last of his cum, he pulls me back onto his lap, his hands roaming over my body.

"Such a dirty girl," he murmurs, kissing my neck. "But so good. So fucking good."

I squirm in his lap, loving the praise and his touch, and the way he's making me feel.

"But if you're feeling better, you need to get back to class. What time is your doctor's appointment? I'll meet you there, baby."

I sigh, wishing I could stay with him. "It's at four."

"Then I'll meet you there, and if it goes well, I can take you home with me, and we can get to work knocking you up."

He's got a devilish grin on his face that makes my heart skip a beat, and I'm practically trembling with excitement as I get up and straighten my clothes.

"Can't wait," I say.

"Me either."

We share a lingering look before I force myself to turn and walk out of his office.

I'm giddy as I hurry to my next class, thinking about what it will be like to be home with him, and knowing that tonight could be the night we conceive a baby, if we haven't succeeded already.

Chapter Six

Shawn:

I can't stop pacing in the waiting area of the doctor's office, and people are giving me strange looks, but I don't care. Katie has been in with the doctor for almost thirty minutes, and I'm having to fight the urge to barge in there and find out what's going on.

Luckily, I don't know anybody in the waiting area. It was a risk to come here and be seen with Katie in public, in case any of the students or professors from the college happened to be here too, but I don't want her having to deal with the appointments on her own.

Could she be pregnant already? She had looked very pale when she'd come to my office earlier, and she said she'd felt nauseous. But surely it's too early for her to be showing symptoms if she is. We only had sex a week ago, after all.

Two conflicting emotions are warring inside me, creating a storm of nerves that has my stomach tied in knots.

Part of me is thrilled by the idea that she could be pregnant already. But another part of me is also disappointed that it might have happened so soon. Only because I had hoped to have a few weeks or months of being intimate with her. Of breeding her in the most primal sense.

If she is knocked up already, she might not want to fuck me anymore, and the knowledge that I might only get that one time inside her is enough to make my chest ache with a painful longing.

I just can't believe how much this young woman has come to mean to me already. She's been constantly in my thoughts over the last few days, and every moment I haven't been able to talk to her, or see her, has been torture.

I already know I'm in way over my head with this, feeling things for her that I really shouldn't be. Once she's had my baby and got the money she needs to help her family, she's going to walk away. And I'll be left alone with the baby. I can't blame her for that, though. It was what I asked for, and I even asked her to sign a contract to that effect.

But I'm starting to think I want much more with Katie than just a legal agreement.

Finally, the door to the doctor's office opens and Katie emerges. She walks over to me and I pull her into my arms.

"Are you?" I ask, holding my breath as I wait for the answer.

"Not yet," she says, and the corners of her lips pull upwards into a smile that doesn't quite reach her eyes. "The test came back negative. I'm not sure what was going on with me earlier. The doctor says I'm perfectly healthy, so I guess that means we can start trying properly now?"

My heart drops to hear she's not pregnant yet, but at least this means I get more time being intimate with her. The thought of it makes my dick twitch as it starts to harden. I'm going to fuck her nonstop until she's knocked up with my baby.

"Let's go," I say, my voice deepening into a growl. "We're going to start right now."

I grab her hand and drag her out of the building, hearing her little whimpers as she is forced to follow behind me. When we get to the car park, I pull her close and dip my head, capturing her lips in a fierce kiss. It won't be long until I've got her in my bed and screaming my name while I'm ruining her tight little cunt, and I can't wait.

Katie moans against my lips, and her hands come up to tangle in my hair. I love how desperate she is for me.

When we break apart, her pupils are dilated and her breathing is labored.

"Let's go," I say again, before kissing her softly and stepping towards my own car. "Follow me back to my place in your car, but drive safely, baby. Okay?"

She nods, her eyes never leaving mine. "Okay."

We part ways, and I quickly make my way back home, eager to get started. I can't stop glancing into the rear-view mirror, making sure she's right behind me. My dick is so fucking hard it's a miracle there's enough blood left circulating around the rest of my body to be able to drive as safely as I am.

When we pull into my driveway, I get out and wait for her, and as soon as she gets out of her car, I'm dragging her towards the house.

"Sir," she gasps, giggling at my urgency. "Slow down!"

"Can't, baby," I mutter, unlocking the front door and pulling her inside. "Need you too much."

The second the door closes behind us, I push her up against it, crushing my lips against hers. My hands are on her waist, pinning her in place. She squirms against me, and the feel of her body rubbing against mine sends a jolt of pleasure through me.

"Want you," I mumble against her lips, grinding my hard cock against her. "Need you."

"Please," she whimpers. "I need you too."

Her fingers claw at my back, trying to pull me even closer.

"Gonna fuck you so hard, baby," I growl, nipping her bottom lip with my teeth. "Gonna fuck you raw."

She moans, her nails digging into my back through my shirt.

"I'm going to fill your tight little pussy with my seed. Get you pregnant. Knock you the fuck up."

She gasps, her hips bucking against mine. "Please, Sir. Yes. Please."

I'm losing control fast, and I know I need to slow down and try to savor the experience, but it's just not possible. The thought of Katie pregnant with my baby, of the two of us raising a child together, is making me crazy.

I can't take it. I need her.

I grab her by the waist and carry her to the couch, throwing her down on the cushions and pinning her down with my body. I kiss her again, hard and rough, and her body responds to my touch. She's trembling beneath me, and when I finally pull away from the kiss, her lips are red and swollen, and her eyes are glassy.

"I know I promised to go slower this time, Katie, but I don't know if I can. I'm too fucking desperate to be inside you again."

"Then don't hold back," she says, her voice a soft whisper. "Give me all you've got, Sir. Fuck me."

Her words send a surge of desire through me, and I kiss her again, roughly claiming her mouth. My hands roam her body, feeling her curves through her clothes, before finding the hem of her shirt and lifting it up, breaking the kiss long enough to get the garment off her.

My mouth finds her neck, and I start to kiss and suck the delicate skin, marking her as mine. She lets out a moan, and her fingers dig into my shoulders.

"More," she pleads, and I happily oblige, my mouth trailing lower until it finds her breasts. I pull the cups of her bra down, revealing her perfect tits, and I take one of the stiff pink nipples into my mouth, sucking on it gently.

She moans again, her back arching off the couch.

"You like that, baby?" I murmur before flicking my tongue across the sensitive bud.

"Yes, Sir," she gasps.

I move to the other breast, giving it the same treatment, while my hand slides down between her legs, pushing her skirt up around her waist. Her panties are soaked, and I can feel her heat through the thin material.

I rub her gently, feeling the way her pussy clenches, and the slick wetness coating her panties.

"Oh God," she moans, her hips bucking against my hand. "Feels so good, Sir."

"That's right, baby," I growl. "Just relax and let me take care of you."

I continue teasing her, stroking her through her panties, and sucking her nipples.

After a few moments, her body starts to tense, and she cries out, her hips bucking wildly as she reaches her climax.

"So beautiful, Katie," I whisper, watching her face as she comes undone.

Her eyes are closed, and her face is flushed, her lips parted in a silent cry. Her body is trembling, and her hands are clutching the cushions beneath her.

I'm captivated by the sight.

Once her orgasm subsides, I sit up and start pulling her panties off her legs. Then I remove the rest of her clothes and admire her naked body.

"So perfect," I murmur.

Her eyes are still closed, and she's still catching her breath, but her legs part slightly, inviting me in.

I quickly shed my own clothes before settling between her thighs, my hard cock rubbing against her soft pussy.

"Oh, Sir," she gasps, her hips bucking. "Please. I need you inside me."

I can't wait any longer, either. My cock is throbbing with need, and I can't resist the urge to sink deep inside her tight little cunt.

I line myself up, and then push into her slowly, inch by inch, watching as my thick shaft disappears into her tiny opening.

"God, Katie, you're so fucking tight," I groan, my hips rocking as I bury myself in her warmth.

"It's... oh fuck. You're so big," she gasps, her hands reaching for my shoulders and holding onto me tightly.

I begin to move, slowly at first, but then faster, the sensation of her velvety walls wrapped around my cock driving me wild. She feels like heaven, and the way she's responding to me is making me lose my mind.

She's moaning and panting, her hips moving in time with mine, and her hands are clawing at my back.

"Harder," she pleads. "Faster. Please, Sir."

"Fuck, Katie," I growl. "You feel so fucking good."

My movements become more erratic as my own orgasm builds, and I can feel her body start to tense again, her pussy tightening around my cock.

"Yes," she cries out, her head thrown back, her eyes squeezed shut. "Oh God, yes. Please, Sir. Make me come. Fill me with your seed. I want your baby inside me so fucking badly."

Hearing her say that is all it takes to push me over the edge, and I explode, filling her with my cum, the force of my climax almost blinding.

She screams, her own release crashing over her, and her body convulses beneath mine.

We stay like that for a moment, both of us trembling and panting, the aftermath of our orgasms coursing through us.

Finally, I roll off her and pull her into my arms, cradling her against my chest.

"Wow," she whispers.

"Yeah," I agree.

I reach down between her thighs, feeling my cum dripping out of her. It's so hot, and the thought of her being full of my seed makes me want to fuck her again.

"Are you sore?" I ask, gently stroking her folds.

"A little," she admits. "But it feels good."

I continue touching her, scooping up the cum that leaks out of her and pushing it back inside her. Each time I fill her with my fingers, she lets out a little moan that has my dick twitching back to life in record time.

"Such a greedy girl," I say, grinning at her.

"I just like knowing your seed is inside me, Sir," she whimpers.

Fuck. I've never met anyone as sexy as her, and I know I'm in trouble. She's going to be the one woman I can't resist; the one to make me question my fear of relationships; and I'm completely powerless to stop it.

I want her to be mine.

I'll just have to show her how good it feels to be with me, so that by the time the baby comes, she won't ever want to leave.

Chapter Seven

Katie:

"Oh, well hello there, stranger," Lexi says with a smirk on her face as I drift to consciousness. "It's not often you sleep in your own bed anymore. When am I going to meet this sex god who won't ever let you leave his bed?"

I rub my eyes before pushing myself up into a sleeping position. My face is burning hot, and I can only imagine how much I must be blushing.

"It's not like that," I protest, even though that's exactly what it's been like.

It's been two weeks since I visited the doctor and got the all clear to start trying for a baby, and practically all my free time has been spent with Shawn. He's determined to knock me up, and it's brought out something feral in him. Something that means he's all over me as soon as we're alone.

And I have to admit, I love that part of him. My pussy is tingling just thinking about it. These past two weeks have been the happiest of my life, and while I'm desperate to get pregnant and give Shawn the baby he wants, I also know I'll be sad once it actually happens. Because then the intimacy between us will have to stop, and I'll miss having him buried deep inside me, fucking me raw and filling me with his cum. And the tender moments afterwards when he holds me in his arms as I drift into an exhausted sleep. It's safe to say that I've fallen for him harder than I ever imagined I could over the last couple of weeks.

I haven't told him any of this, and I'm not planning to. It'll just make things awkward. We've got contracts in place, and I know he's only looking for a surrogate - not for a wife and mother for his child. If I tell him how I feel, he might cut our arrangement off completely, and I don't want that.

"Will you be home again tonight?" Lexi asks. "I was thinking we could watch a movie together or something?"

I wince inwardly. Today is Shawn's birthday, and we've got plans to have dinner together at his house. Of course, we can't really go out anywhere special to celebrate, no matter how much I'd love to do that, because there is just too much of a risk of us being seen together.

"I'm so sorry," I say, and the way the smile falls from Lexi's face makes my heart ache. "I've got plans tonight. But if you want, I can keep my weekend clear and we can spend the entire two days doing whatever you want. I promise."

I'll miss Shawn, but I love Lexi too, and I've been missing my time with her. Besides, my period is due any day now, so it's not like I'll be fertile this weekend. So I doubt he'll mind me taking a weekend with my best friend.

Lexi sighs, but then the corners of her lips tug upwards into a small smile. "Fine. But I'm going to hold you to that. We're going to do whatever I want, even if I want to go bungee jumping or whatever, okay?"

I laugh and lean over to hug her. "Okay. Just try not to pick anything too crazy."

"No promises," she says, laughing as she rises from where she's sitting on the edge of the bed. "I'm heading to the library. I've got an assignment I need to finish before college starts."

"Okay, I'll see you later. Meet for lunch at the cafeteria like normal?"

She nods and waves, then grabs her bag and heads out.

I flop back onto the bed, smiling as I think about my plans later with Shawn. My entire body flushes with warmth at the thought of spending time with him, and I know I've got to stop this before my feelings grow even stronger. I can't afford to fall in love with him. Not when I'm just the woman he's using to have his baby.

An idea pops into my head and I sit upright fast enough that it makes my head spin a little. What if I could tell him today that I'm pregnant? Surely that would be the perfect gift for him on his birthday.

I reach under the bed, digging around until I find the box wrapped in a plastic bag. My heart starts beating harder in my chest as I pull out the pregnancy test and start reading the instructions. It says that it should be effective from the day my period is due, so that means that the test should work today.

The idea of surprising him with this is so exciting, and it's going to make his day even more special.

I rush to the bathroom and pee on the stick, before setting a timer on my phone and rushing to get dressed. There's no way I can stay still right now, not with all this adrenaline coursing through my veins.

As I'm getting dressed, my phone timer goes off and I hurry back to the bathroom.

My heart is pounding and my hands are shaking, but I manage to pick the stick up and look at the result.

Positive.

A rush of elation flows through me and I jump up and down, clapping my hands.

I'm pregnant.

With Shawn's baby.

This is going to be the best birthday present for him.

I try to push down the other feelings - the ones that want to bring tears to my eyes that the intimate phase of our journey together is most likely going to be over now. Today is Shawn's special day, and he deserves to spend it being happy. He deserves a family, and now he's going to get the baby he's always wanted.

I carefully wrap the test up and tuck it into a gift bag. Now I just have to decide if I want to wait until tonight to tell him, or if I should go and see him right now.

After pacing back and forth a few times, I decide that I want to tell him sooner rather than later. There's no way I can possibly focus on anything else today.

Grabbing my keys, I hurry out of the apartment and begin the short walk to campus. It's a little early, but I know he usually gets to the office around this time to grade papers and prepare for his day before the first lesson. It seems like the perfect time to tell him. Then he can spend the whole of his birthday happy with the knowledge that I'm carrying his baby.

I can't wait to see his face when I tell him!

Chapter Eight

Shawn:

"Hey, Professor Adams. Are you busy right now?"

I glance up from the paper I'm marking and smile when I see Katie standing in the doorway of my office. Her cheeks are flushed and her eyes are bright and excited, and her presence immediately brings a smile to my face.

"I'm never too busy for you," I say.

I wait until she's entered the room and closed the door before I rise from my chair, rushing over to her so I can pull her into my arms and claim her mouth with a deep kiss. Just seeing her has got me instantly hard, and the urge to lay her out across my desk and drive my dick into the soft, welcoming heat between her thighs is almost too much.

Katie melts against me, her lips parting easily so I can explore her mouth. My tongue brushes against hers, and the sweet taste of her drives me wild.

I reluctantly break the kiss and take a step back. My hands rest on her shoulders and I look her over.

"What are you doing here?" I ask, unable to hide the joy in my voice. "I thought we were seeing each other tonight?"

"Oh, we are," she says, bouncing a little on the balls of her feet.

I tilt my head to the side as I watch her with curiosity. I'm not sure I've ever seen her this excited before, and it's fucking adorable. It's only then that I notice the gift bag she's holding.

"It's for you," she says, a wide grin on her face as she holds the bag out to me.

"Me?"

I take the bag from her, my heart starting to beat faster. No one has given me a gift in... I'm not sure how long. It's a kind of sad realization, but the way Katie is watching me, her eyes full of happiness, helps distract me from the pang of loneliness that threatens to wash over me.

"It's a special gift," she tells me, her grin never fading. "For your birthday."

"Katie, you didn't have to get me anything," I murmur. "You know, just letting me ravage your body all night would have been more than enough."

I wink at her, and her smile widens even more while a blush creeps up her neck to turn her face a cute shade of pink.

"Well, you can still do that if you want, Sir. But I thought this gift would help to make your day extra special."

She's practically buzzing, and I've never seen anything as sexy and cute at the same time.

I walk around the desk and take a seat in my office chair, then pat my lap. In a heartbeat, she's seated on my thighs, her legs dangling over the side of the arm rest.

"I can't wait to see your face when you open it," she says.

I can hear the excitement in her voice, and it makes my own heart beat even faster. Whatever is in this bag, it's something that has got her worked up, and she wants to share it with me. That makes whatever it is even more special.

Slowly, I open the gift bag and reach inside, pulling out a small wrapped item. I pull away the tissue paper and find myself looking at a pregnancy test.

For a moment, I'm too shocked to react. Then, I pick the test up, looking closer at the results.

Two pink lines.

"We're having a baby," she says softly, and I can hear the emotion in her voice. "Happy birthday, Sir!"

"We're having a baby," I repeat, as if trying the words out on my tongue.

My heart feels like it's going to burst right out of my chest, and the feeling is incredible. All these years of wishing I could have a baby, and now Katie is finally giving me the best gift anyone has ever given me.

I can't resist the urge to kiss her again, and my mouth crashes against hers. My hands grip her hips, holding her close.

"Thank you," I whisper, kissing along her jaw and down her neck. "I don't think I've ever been this happy before."

"Me either," she replies, and her voice is shaky.

I pull back and look at her. She's smiling, but I can see the sadness in her eyes.

"Is everything okay?" I ask.

She nods quickly, blinking back tears.

"Everything is perfect," she assures me.

"You can talk to me," I say, brushing a stray strand of hair away from her face. "You know that, right? If there's something upsetting you, I want to help."

Katie swallows and takes a deep breath.

"It's just going to be weird, once I'm pregnant, not seeing you as much as I do now. I mean, I know I'll still see you for doctor's appointments and stuff, but I guess I've just got used to being with you every spare moment I've had, and I'm going to miss that, Sir."

I cup her face in my hands and tilt her head upwards so she's looking into my eyes. "What if I told you I didn't want that to end?" I say, my voice thick with emotion. "That I want you to be more than just a surrogate to me?"

Katie blinks rapidly, and I can see the tears threatening to spill out over her cheeks. "Really?" she breathes.

"Really."

Katie lunges towards me, flinging her arms around my neck and crashing her lips against mine. I return her kiss, tangling one hand in her hair while the other slides down her body to grab her ass, grinding her against my already aching erection.

I've never been so turned on by a kiss before, but with her, everything is different. She's the most perfect woman I've ever met, and she's going to be the mother of my child. This woman who is going to make all of my dreams come true.

She grinds her hips down, rubbing herself against the bulge in my pants. Her movements are desperate, and she whimpers into my mouth.

"I need you, Sir," she moans against my lips.

I let out a growl and grip her hips, lifting her for a moment before sitting her down on my desk. "Don't worry, baby. I'm going to take such good care of you."

With quick movements, I begin unbuttoning her shirt, tugging at the material in my eagerness to get her naked. Her bra is next to go, and I pause to cup her breasts in my hands. The breasts that are already so damn perfect, but that will soon be growing bigger when she'll begin producing the milk that will nourish our baby.

I lean down and capture a nipple in my mouth, sucking and flicking the hard nub with my tongue. My fingers tease her other nipple, rolling the bud and pinching it.

Katie arches her back, thrusting her breasts closer to my face. Her hands are in my hair, tugging at the short strands as she holds me against her chest.

I give her other nipple the same attention, making sure they are both thoroughly licked and sucked before continuing my path down her body. When I reach her stomach, I stop there to kiss and lick at her soft skin, knowing that soon enough, it will be swelling with my baby that's growing inside her. At the same time, my fingers are pushing her skirt up around her waist and pulling her panties down.

"I'm going to spend the next nine months worshipping every fucking inch of your perfect, fertile body, baby," I groan between kisses. "You've made me so fucking happy, and I'm going to do everything I can to make sure you're just as happy as I am."

Katie moans as I trail kisses over her abdomen, then down to her pussy. My fingers run through her slit, teasing her entrance and spreading her juices around. She's already so wet for me, and her body is trembling under my touch.

"I'm already happy," she breathes, her hands fisting the material of my shirt as she tries to hold on to me. "Because I'm with you."

Fuck.

I feel like the luckiest man in the world right now, and the desire to take care of this girl has never been so strong.

I bury my face between her legs, licking and sucking at her clit while I plunge two fingers deep inside her. She tastes fucking amazing, and I groan as I lick at her folds. My free hand slides up her body, gripping her breast and teasing the hard, sensitive nipple.

Her breathing is ragged and her hands are clutching desperately at my hair, and she's making the hottest fucking noises. She's so responsive to my touch, and her body is practically vibrating with the need to come.

"Sir," she pants. "Please, Sir."

Her hips lift, pressing her pussy harder against my mouth. She's dripping wet, and her sweet nectar is running down my chin.

"Do you need to come, baby?" I murmur against her clit, blowing a stream of air across the sensitive bud and enjoying the way she shudders and cries out.

"Yes, Sir. Please. I'm so close."

Her legs are spread wide, her feet planted on the edge of the desk so she can thrust herself against my face, and the sight of her like this is so fucking erotic.

"Come for me, Katie," I say, returning my tongue to her clit. "Come all over my face, baby."

But before I can lower my mouth back to her clit, there is a knock at the door that sends us both scrambling to straighten ourselves out.

"Fuck," I mutter under my breath.

Katie grabs her clothes and crawls into the knee-well of my desk to hide from whoever is outside the door, while I wipe frantically at my mouth with the back of my hand to remove the glistening traces of her arousal.

I crouch down, bringing myself eye-to-eye with Katie.

"You get dressed, baby. I'll go and talk to them outside, okay?"

She nods quickly, and I stand, walking towards the door to find out who was rude enough to interrupt my time with my girl.

Chapter Nine

Katie:

By the time Shawn gets back to his office, I'm fully dressed and curled up in his chair, hugging my knees to my chest as I fight back tears.

"What's wrong?" he asks, sounding surprised to see me looking so upset.

"I've changed my mind," I say, flinching as the words rip a hole in my heart. Or that's how it feels, at least.

Shawn rushes to my side and crouches beside the chair, and with a tentative hand, he reaches out to stroke my hair back, away from my face.

"About what?" he asks, and when I glance up at his face, he looks completely bewildered.

And, to be fair, he's not the only one feeling confused. Before the knock on the door just now, I'd felt like the happiest woman in the world. But when it had sunk in what we were really doing - something that could end with Shawn in a lot of trouble and with me being kicked out of college - it all suddenly felt like too much.

Do I really want a relationship that could have such dire consequences for us both? A relationship where we would have to hide our feelings for each other and I would be nothing more than a dirty little secret for him?

Sure, I should have thought about these things before now, but it had been easier to get carried away when I wasn't carrying his child inside me. If I'm honest, the consequences hadn't meant much to me at the time. But now, it all feels much more serious. And the way we'd both rushed to hide what was happening when there was a knock on the door had been a bitter reminder that, even with the baby in the picture, this couldn't be anything more than an exciting fling.

When I don't say anything for a long time, Shawn speaks again.

"Tell me what's going on, baby. If I know what's wrong, I can fix it. Do you mean you changed your mind about the baby?"

A bitter laugh escapes me. "It's a little late for that, don't you think?"

I wrap my arms around my stomach, as if it will help me protect the little life inside me, and I sigh heavily.

"I don't regret the baby," I say slowly as I try to work out what it is I want to say. "I guess I've just been so caught up in the excitement of being with you after having a crush on you for so long, and I forgot to think about things in the long term. I'm happy that I can give you the baby you want so badly, but I'm sad I didn't protect my heart. I fell head over heels for you, and I failed to recognize that any relationship we have would be hidden away. But I don't want that, Shawn. Not when I'm crazy about you."

I'm barely holding myself together as the words fall out, and it hurts. It feels like my heart is being ripped in two, and I know it's stupid, but I can't help it. I love this man, and being without him will break my heart.

Shawn stands, and my breath catches as I wait to see what he's going to say. He walks to the door, and for a second, my heart sinks and I fear that he's leaving.

Instead, he locks the door and walks back to me.

He scoops me up in his arms and sets me back down on his desk, grabbing a handful of my hair in his fist and using it to tilt my head up. When my eyes meet his, I gasp. There's a fire in his eyes, and it makes my heart beat faster and sends a thrill rushing through my veins.

"I'm sorry, baby. I should have been clearer. This was a huge mistake."

I open my mouth to speak, but he cuts me off with a searing kiss that makes me melt. There's a little voice in the back of my head telling me that I should put a stop to this, but his lips on mine feel so damn good that I can't fight it.

He pulls back and continues talking, sounding as breathless as I feel.

"What I meant was, it was a huge mistake for me not to tell you about my feelings sooner. Katie, I don't just want you as a surrogate or a fling. I want you as my girlfriend. As my partner. As the mother of my children. And as the woman who shares my bed every single night."

My heart is racing so fast, and the room seems to be spinning.

"Are you serious?" I ask.

I need him to say the words, need him to spell it out for me.

"As a heart attack," he replies. "I love you, Katie. You're perfect. I knew that from the moment I first met you, but spending all this time with you has just made me realize how special you are. You're gorgeous, funny, smart, and a million other amazing things. I should have told you sooner how much I cared about you, but I was worried that maybe you didn't feel the same way."

He dips his head and brushes feather-light kisses against the corner of my mouth. "You're mine, Katie. That was inevitable from the moment you turned up on my doorstep. We only have to keep our relationship a secret for a couple more months, until you leave college, and then I promise you that I'll be shouting about my love for you from the fucking rooftops, okay? Can you handle that, baby? Waiting just a few more months before the whole world knows you're mine?"

I nod, my heart soaring. "I can wait," I assure him. "So long as I know we won't have to hide this forever. But what about the contracts we signed? And the money I was going to give my parents? Oh god, if I don't help them, they're still going to lose the house."

"Shhhh, baby," Shawn whispers, capturing my face in his large hands as the panic starts rising up inside me. "It's okay. I'm going to take care of all of that, Katie. You have my word that your family are not going to end up on the streets. Right now, all you have to worry about is keeping that little baby inside you safe and warm. Everything else is my responsibility."

Tears fill my eyes, and I blink rapidly to try and stop them from falling.

"You're too good to be true," I tell him.

His lips capture mine again, and I'm so overwhelmed by everything he's just said, and by the way he's looking at me. His eyes are filled with a look of pure adoration, and I can't believe how lucky I am.

He loves me. He wants a future with me. And we're going to have a baby together.

"I'm the luckiest man in the world, Katie. You make me so fucking happy, and I'm never going to let anything hurt you, I promise."

"I love you, Sir," I whisper.

"I love you too, baby."

This time, when he kisses me, I feel a rush of heat flood through me, and I realize that we didn't actually finish what we started earlier.

"Make love to me, Shawn," I whisper, my fingers lacing through his hair. "Please, I need you."

He lets out a low growl. "I need you too, baby. But I don't want to risk any more interruptions."

Before my lower lip can even form into a pout, Shawn chuckles. "Go to my house and wait for me there. I should only be a few minutes behind you. I'm going to get out of all my lectures today so I can spend my entire birthday with the woman I love."

Shawn reaches into his pocket and pulls out a key. "This is for my house," he says, before pausing for a moment. "No, sorry. I meant, this is for *our* house."

My heart is racing as I take the key from him, and he grins down at me.

"Don't start without me," he warns, a playful edge to his tone. "I want to be the one to make you come repeatedly today, and it's my birthday, so surely you can't deny me that."

I shake my head. "No, Sir. I won't start without you."

He helps me off his desk, and my legs are still a little shaky. But the butterflies in my stomach have nothing to do with nerves, and everything to do with the excitement of knowing Shawn will be home soon.

Home. Something about that feels so right, and it's got nothing to do with the house itself. It's Shawn that makes it feel like home.

"Be careful," he says, cupping my cheek. "I'll see you in a few minutes, okay?"

I nod and stand up on tiptoes, kissing him one last time.

When I pull back, I smile widely up at him. "Happy birthday, Sir. See you soon."

He winks. "Oh, trust me, baby. I'll be joining you as quickly as possible."

Chapter Ten

Shawn:

By the time I get home, Katie is already sprawled out on the bed, stripped naked and looking every inch the delicious snack I know she is. A groan escapes me as my dick suddenly gets even harder, which I would have thought was impossible a few moments ago.

I've been rock hard all the way home, knowing that things are different between us now. This is the start of our lives together. The start of our journey to becoming a family, and it's everything I could have wanted.

I strip off as quickly as possible, and Katie watches my every movement with a smile on her face and lust in her eyes. She's so fucking sexy, and it takes all the willpower I have not to just climb onto the bed and thrust inside her.

"Come here," she says softly, stretching her arms above her head and arching her back. "It feels like I've been waiting forever for you, Sir, and I need you inside me."

"Fuck," I groan. "Baby, you are so damn hot."

I climb onto the bed and lay myself on top of her, keeping my weight on my elbows so I don't hurt her or the precious life inside her. My cock presses against her dripping center, and it feels so fucking good that I can't hold back a moan of pleasure.

"I can't believe how fucking beautiful you are," I murmur, kissing a path from her collarbone down her chest and across the soft, supple flesh of her breasts.

She's breathing hard and her chest is heaving, and the way her body responds to me is so fucking hot.

I tease the nipple of her left breast, taking it into my mouth and sucking hard before scraping my teeth over the sensitive bud.

"Sir," she cries out.

She sounds like she's pleading, and it's such a beautiful sound. I know what she needs, and I'm desperate to give it to her. But this moment feels so perfect that I want to draw it out and savor every second of it.

She's mine now, and for the rest of our lives, so there's no need to rush anything.

I move back up to her mouth and claim her lips in a slow, sensual kiss. Her soft whimpers spill against my lips, and the needy little sound drives me wild. I slide a hand down her body and cup her pussy, dipping one finger into her welcoming heat.

"You're so wet for me, baby," I groan. "Fuck, it feels so good to know how much you want me."

Her hips lift, urging me on, and she looks up at me, her eyes wide and trusting.

"Please, Sir," she murmurs.

"What is it, baby? What do you need?"

"I need to feel you inside me," she whispers.

A teasing grin tugs at the corners of my lips. "But I am inside you, baby."

Katie lets out a frustrated groan and her mouth turns downwards into an adorable pout. "That isn't what I meant, Sir. I need your cock. Please."

She looks up at me with those beautiful eyes, and I know I can't resist her when she's begging like this.

"Okay, baby," I reply, pressing a kiss to the tip of her nose. "You've given me the world today, so you can have whatever you want."

I pull my finger out of her and line myself up at her entrance before burying myself inside her in one long, smooth motion. She gasps and moans, and the sound is like music to my ears.

"You feel so fucking good, baby," I murmur.

I'm so overcome with emotion that it takes me a second to gather myself, and she wriggles her hips beneath me.

"Please, Sir," she whines. "You're teasing me."

"Oh, am I?" I reply.

She nods and bites her lip, and it's so fucking sexy.

"Tell me what you want, baby. Beg for it."

"I need to feel your cock, Sir. Hard and fast. Please, give it to me. Fuck me until I'm screaming."

Her words go straight to my cock, and a rush of desire courses through me.

I start to move, pulling back before thrusting deep again, and she moans, arching her spine and bucking her hips. I wrap my arm around her waist and hold her close, my mouth claiming hers again as we find our rhythm.

"I love you," I whisper.

She's looking up at me, and it feels so intense, and yet somehow not enough.

"I love you too, Shawn," she replies.

There's a sincerity in her tone, and a fire in her eyes, and it's perfect.

We move together, lost in each other, and nothing has ever felt more right. We're meant to be together. We're meant to be a family. And now, nothing is standing in our way.

Katie is mine, and I'm going to cherish her for the rest of my life.

Our bodies rock together, and Katie digs her nails into my back as she wraps her legs around my waist. Her walls tighten around me, and I know she's close.

"That's it, baby," I urge. "Come for me. Let me hear how much you love this."

"Yes, Sir," she cries. "Please, please, please. Don't stop."

Her words are barely coherent, but I can tell she's right on the edge.

"Do it, baby. Come on my cock. I need to feel you."

I'm desperate for her. Every part of me is burning with a need to be closer, deeper, and it's incredible. I've never felt like this before, and it's so fucking intense.

"Shawn," she cries, her whole body shaking as her orgasm overtakes her.

"Good girl," I whisper.

Her pussy clamps around me, and I can't hold back anymore. My own release barrels through me, and I cry out, emptying myself inside her.

We stay locked together, our chests heaving as we try to catch our breath.

"Holy shit," Katie says, sounding dazed.

"I know," I reply, grinning at her.

I brush her hair back from her face and stare down at her, loving the sight of her flushed cheeks and the satisfied smile on her lips. I make a silent vow to myself that I'll do whatever it takes to keep her looking this happy for the rest of her life.

"Are you okay, baby?"

She nods. "That was incredible."

"You're incredible."

I pull out of her, and the whimper that falls from her lips almost makes me want to slide straight back in. I settle for leaning down and kissing her.

"Don't worry, baby," I say, my tone light. "There's plenty more where that came from."

She giggles, and it's the sweetest sound. "Promise?"

"Oh, trust me, Katie. It's a fucking promise."

A promise to give her whatever she desires for the rest of her life. Because she's already given me everything I could ever want and so much more.

Epilogue

Katie:

One year later:

"There's my sweet little baby!" Mom coos as soon as I open the front door and she sees I'm holding baby Anna in my arms.

I laugh and hand Anna over, knowing it's only a matter of time before she's taken from me, anyway.

"I really appreciate you offering to watch her for a couple of hours while I rest, Mom," I say, a tired smile on my face. "Anna kept me up most of last night with her teething, and I'm exhausted."

"No problem," she says, smiling widely, although her eyes never leave her granddaughter's face. "I'm happy to help out at any time. Besides, your brothers and sisters all love her just as much as I do, so they all lend a hand as well."

I hand her the diaper bag, and lean in to give Anna a kiss on one of her pudgy little cheeks. "I'll miss you, baby girl," I whisper, even though she's too young to understand what I'm saying.

"I'll bring her back after dinner," Mom says, already making her way down the pathway to make the short walk to their house. "That should give you plenty of time to rest."

"Thank you so much," I say again, but all I get in response is a wave over her shoulder as she's walking away.

I gently close the front door and turn to see Shawn walking up behind me. "Your idea to buy them a house just down the street was genius," I say, snuggling into the warmth of his body as he wraps his strong arms around me. "Having their help has been a godsend."

He chuckles and kisses the top of my head. "I am full of good ideas. And my next one is that you need to get your butt to bed, baby. You need some rest."

I pout and take a step back, grabbing his hands in mine as I start walking backwards towards the stairs.

"I'll go to bed if you come with me."

He laughs and shakes his head, but follows me anyway.

"You're supposed to be resting," he chastises. "Maybe I need to give you a spanking for not taking a nap when you get a chance."

The mere mention of a spanking has my pussy clenching. I haven't had one of those for a long time, and the idea of Shawn taking me over his knee is wonderfully appealing.

"Well, Mom said she isn't going to bring Anna back until after dinner, so by my calculations, there is time for a spanking, a fucking and a nap. I mean, this is the first time we've had any proper alone time since Anna was born. Shouldn't we make the most of it?"

He lets out a low growl. "You make a good point, baby. It would be almost criminal to waste this opportunity."

"I have some good ideas sometime too, you know."

Shawn laughs and bends to wrap his arms around my thighs, before lifting me and draping me over his broad shoulder.

"Oh, I know you do. And the best idea you ever had was to reply to that ad last year. It brought us together, and now you're all mine."

I grin to myself as I hang upside down over his shoulder, my body jolting slightly as he takes the steps two at a time.

It was a pretty good idea, even if I do say so myself, and I'm so grateful I took that chance. Now I'm married to an amazing man who made good on his promise to take care of me and my family. And I've got the baby I always hoped I'd have one day.

Life couldn't get any better than this.

About The Author

Willow Watkins is a British author who has been obsessed with reading romances ever since she was a teenager. This love of reading has blossomed into an addiction to crafting her own love stories. Very spicy love stories, of course. Things always taste better with a bit of spice added, don't you think?

If you'd like to stalk her online, check out the following link: **https://allmylinks.com/willow-watkins**